SPOOKS A

A weekend on the river is the setting for this hilarious follow-up to *Spook Spotting* – and as usual Amy and her wild imagination go overboard!

Mary Hooper knows more than most people what makes a good story – she's had over six hundred published in teenage and women's magazines, from *Just Seventeen* to *Woman's Own*, and she has tutored evening classes in Creative Writing. In addition, she's the highly regarded author of over fifty titles for young people, including another about Amy and Hannah, *Spook Spotting*.

Books by the same author

Spook Spotting

For older readers

Best Friends, Worst Luck
The Boyfriend Trap
Mad About the Boy
The Peculiar Power of Tabitha Brown

MARY HOOPER

Illustrations by
SUSAN HELLARD

WALKER BOOKS
AND SUBSIDIARIES
LONDON • BOSTON • SYDNEY

First published 1997 by Walker Books Ltd
87 Vauxhall Walk, London SE11 5HJ

This edition published 1999

2 4 6 8 10 9 7 5 3 1

This book has been typeset in Plantin.

Printed in England by Clays Ltd, St Ives plc

British Library Cataloguing in Publication Data
A catalogue record for this book
is available from the British Library.

ISBN 0-7445-7260-6

Contents

1. Before the Weekend 7

2. Friday Morning 15

3. Friday Afternoon 25

4. Friday Evening 33

5. Friday Night 43

6. Saturday Morning...........................51

7. Saturday Afternoon.........................61

8. Saturday Evening............................73

9. Sunday Morning..............................83

Chapter 1

Before the Weekend

....

I was slouching in the armchair, reading, when I heard Mum's key in the front door. Immediately I heaved myself up and ran with my book to the window. I positioned myself on the sill, half in and half out, and carried on reading.

She came in with her cross, outdoor face on. The face she wears when she's been working all day, the train's arrived late and she's had to stand all the way home.

"Amy, you haven't been sitting here All Afternoon, have you?" she said – and that's just how she said it, with capital letters. "Haven't you had any Fresh Air?"

"I *am* having Fresh Air," I pointed out. "Look! Most of me is out of the window and breathing Air Freshly."

"But why don't you go into the garden properly?" Mum said. "Or out for a nice walk or over to see Hannah? Get some exercise."

"I'm just finishing this book," I said.

Mum rolled her eyes.

"Shall I get you a cup of tea?" I asked.

She gave an exaggerated gasp of surprise and collapsed sideways into a chair, so I went into the kitchen to play kind-and-thoughtful-daughters. It was half term and it was the usual thing – Mum was feeling guilty because she'd been at work all week and hadn't seen much of me. She hadn't been able to prod me into Fresh Air and Exercise.

When I came back in with the tea, though, she was sitting up and taking notice, looking almost normal.

"I've got a surprise for you," she said. "At the weekend, you'll be getting a whole lot of fresh air and fun. And so will I."

"Oh yes?" I said a bit cagily. Mum's idea of fun and my idea of fun are not usually the same.

"Guess what I've done?" She beamed. "I've booked us a boat for a long weekend!"

"Ooh!" I said. This did, actually, sound as if it might be quite fun. I'd just finished reading a book of short stories about spooky mysteries on the high seas. It featured ghosts of long-drowned smugglers, phantom ships, mermaids and notes in bottles leading to buried treasure on islands. So I knew the sort of thing that could happen.

"I've already rung Hannah's mum and dad and asked her along."

"Will it be a ship on the high, cruel seas?" I asked eagerly.

"Not exactly," Mum said, sipping her tea.

As she sipped, a selection of weekends with different boaty adventures went through my head: a smugglers yo-ho-ho sort of one, swiftly followed by a secret-grotto-beneath-the-waves one, a herd-of-white-horses-rising-out-of-the-foam one and a mysterious-creatures-from-the-deep-devouring-the-earth one.

But it wasn't any of these.

"It's on a narrow boat," Mum said, putting

down her empty cup and rummaging in her bag for the brochure.

"What d'you mean? How narrow?" I asked.

"No, a *narrowboat*," she said. "That's what they're called."

I frowned. "Well, why can't we have a wider one? Why can't we have a *fattyboat*?"

"Because there aren't such things as *fattyboats*." She passed me the brochure and pointed at a picture. "They were made narrow especially to go up and down canals – although the one we're having is on a river."

"Hmm," I said, looking at the picture and trying to assess the adventure potential of such a small, thin boat. "Will we be *near* the high seas?"

Mum rolled her eyes again. "No, we won't."

"But all rivers run into the sea, don't they?"

"Yes, but miles and miles away."

"Even so..." I nibbled my lip thoughtfully. If the river ran into the sea, then the sea ran into the river, and it stood to reason that anything that was in the sea could get into the river. So that meant that mermaids, trunks of treasure, an old man with a big fork thing and any number of phantom ships looming out of the mist could quite possibly be found on a river. In fact, rivers were probably chock-a-block with such stuff. All the treasure and mermaids could have been swooshed in on a big wave and be unable to find their way out again.

I looked at the picture on the front of the brochure. The narrowboat was black and shiny and looked a bit like a submarine except that it had red and white flowers painted on the side. It was called the *Dark Lady* which I thought was a good, mysterious sort of name. There were photographs of the boat's interior and it had everything – and I mean everything – but in a very narrow sort of way. Like there was a narrowbedroom and a narrowkitchen and a narrowbath with narrowloo and a narrowsitting-room with two narrowseats and a narrowtelly. It looked all right.

I went to ring Hannah; I wanted to find out if she knew anything about spooky seafaring adventures.

She didn't. All she knew about (surprise, surprise) was birds, the sort you might find near a river: ducks and swans and geese and coots and moorhens and herons and suchlike.

"I'm really quite keen," she said when she'd finished telling me all about the wetland habitat of the Corncrake. "I've never had an opportunity to study waterfowl before."

I couldn't stop myself from yawning. How could someone be so interested in feathery, pecky, *boring* things? How could *anyone* be a birdwatcher? But then I forgot about birds and thought about the *Dark Lady* gliding through misty, uncharted waters, and started to get excited.

Chapter 2

Friday Morning

"As it's the end of the season, most of our boats are in dry dock for maintenance," the boatyard man said, "but I think this one will suit you."

We were sitting in what he'd called an office, but which looked more like a shed. He pointed out of the window towards a bright orange boat with green-painted windows called the *Cheeky Chappie*. I hid a shudder. Such colours. Such a name.

"Isn't there one called the *Dark Lady*?" I asked. "Can't we have a shadowy and mysterious sort of boat?"

He gave me an odd look. An *Is-she-raving?* look. "No, I'm afraid you can't," he said. He looked at Mum. "Now, if your husband would like to come aboard with me, I'll show him how the boat operates."

Mum smiled sweetly and falsely. "I don't

happen to have a husband," she said, "so perhaps you'd like to show me, instead."

Mr Boatyard looked taken aback. "It's just the three of you, then. Three females?"

"Afraid so," Mum said in her dangerous voice, and if she'd been a cat all her fur would have been standing on end right down her back.

"Oh dear," he said. "Perhaps I should have found you an easier boat." He pointed to a dark green one called the *Esmerelda* which was standing in the next bay to the *Cheeky Chappie*. "There are only these two – all the others are out of commission. The *Esmerelda* is slower and hasn't a light on the front, as the other one has, but..."

"We'll have the one you first selected, thank you," Mum said frostily. "I've been on a canal holiday before; I'm quite capable of handling something challenging."

"You see," Mr Boatyard said, digging a grave for himself, "I find that women sometimes have trouble in manipulating the tiller correctly – you have to push it to the right to go left and—"

"*If* you don't mind," Mum interrupted, as Hannah and I exchanged gleeful glances. "Perhaps you'd just give me the key so we can get started."

They went aboard the *CC*, as I preferred to think of it, and Hannah and I were given the job of transferring all our gear from Mum's car. The car was going to be left in the car park and then, when we got to the boatyard at the other end of our journey, we'd be driven back to it.

As we carried boxes and bags and books, Hannah and I discussed the various adventures we'd be having soon. At least, I discussed them and she listened.

"They do say," I said, "that mermaids sit on rocks in the sea combing their hair and singing. And when they sing it makes sailors go off course to listen and then they go on the rocks and get shipwrecked."

"I don't think you'll find any mermaids in

this river," Hannah said. "Or shipwrecks."

"And they do say as well," I carried on regardlessly, "that there's millions and trillions of gold bars buried beneath the sea."

"Yes, well, beneath the *sea*," Hannah said.

I took a deep breath. "And another thing they say is that if an albatross circles a ship then it means horribly bad luck and..."

"Albatross?" Hannah said, brightening up. "Large bird often of pure white plumage. Rarely approaches land."

"Mmm..." I said, and went on, "Did you know that once there was thought to be a whole country under the ocean? It was called Atlantis and..."

"Ready?" Mum called to us, still in a frosty voice because Mr Boatyard was around. "Have you two got everything on board?"

"Nearly!" I replied and ran back to the car.

I piled a mass of stuff in my arms to clear it: loo rolls, tea towels, shampoo and toothpaste, books and wellies, things like that. I locked the doors and was just going across from the landing stage on to the boat when there was a blur of brown and white as a dog shot out across my path – and tripped me up. Just deliberately tripped me.

So it wasn't *my* fault that the stuff in my arms went *whoosh splash glug* into the river. Disappeared into a watery grave, as you might say.

I screamed, Hannah screamed, Mum looked round and said, "Oh, *Amy*!" and Mr Boatyard heard it all and called, "I'm not surprised. I hope that child is going to wear a life-jacket."

"Get in here at once!" Mum snapped.

"It wasn't my fault," I said indignantly, handing over the car keys, loo rolls, a book and a welly that I'd saved. "That dog just dashed out of the office – I reckon it's been specially trained to trip people up."

Mum looked round for one last glower at Mr Boatyard, who was standing at the window in his office staring at us.

"Well, what we haven't got we'll just have

to manage without," she said. "I'm casting off. The sooner I can get away the better I'll like it."

She twiddled with something, moved something else and suddenly the whole boat was going forward.

"Hurray!" I said. "Good old Mum!" I knew it was girlie-crawly but I could hardly believe I'd got off so lightly. I thought she'd have made much more fuss about all the stuff going into the river.

"Hurray!" I said again, more loudly. I looked back to the office with a smug *See!-Nah!-She's-done-all-right!* expression, and Mr Boatyard was waving at us.

"He's yelling something," I said to Mum. "I think it's 'Come back!'"

"He'll be lucky," Mum said. "I have no intention of going back." She smiled grimly. "Especially as I don't know how to reverse."

"Can we unpack? Can we explore?" I asked. "Do you want to choose your bed, Hannah?"

Hannah was staring intently at the shore. "I do believe that's a tufted duck."

"Pass my handbag, will you, Amy," Mum said. "I want to put the car keys in it."

I looked round at the piles of stuff lying in the end bit of the boat. "Where is it?"

"It was on the front seat of the car."

"Well, everything that was there is on board," I said. "Every single thing. Except the stuff that..."

Mum let out a scream. "Except the stuff you dropped in the river! You've lost my handbag!"

"I didn't!" I blustered. "I ... it was the dog. It was trained to trip people up. That Mr Boatyard makes it do it!"

"Everything! My credit cards, cheque book, make-up, addresses – oh, I don't believe it! What a *brilliant* start to the weekend!"

Mum, stony-faced and furious, gave the tiller a shove and the boat lurched violently sideways. I stole a look back at Mr Boatyard.

He was in the window waving his fist as much as to say the boat shouldn't be lurching and she was a useless driver.

I thought it best not to point this out to Mum. I beckoned to Hannah and, very quietly, we slipped downstairs. Or below deck, as we sailors say. The spooky seafaring adventures could start any time they liked.

Chapter 3

Friday Afternoon

....

"It's just lucky that I've got a few pounds in my pocket," Mum said, "or we'd have to turn back." She looked at me crossly. "Honestly, it's typical of you, Amy. *So* clumsy."

"It was the dog," I muttered.

"As it is, I don't know how we'll manage. Exactly what have we got with us in the way of food?"

I spread it out on the small table in the room that was a sitting-room and dining-room and which could also be a bedroom if you were desperate. We'd been sailing for a couple of hours and were moored by the bank. Hannah was on deck looking at something which quacked and I was inside trying to look as if I wasn't hungry.

"There's five thick slices of bread, two tins of beans, a couple of eggs and a tin of sardines," I said, trying to make it sound like a feast.

"I *knew* I should have gone shopping on the way to the boatyard," Mum said in her crossest voice. "But I thought it might be fun to buy things at the riverside shops. I *also* thought it would be fun to moor up in the evenings and eat in pubs." She looked at me icily. "But it's going to be a bit difficult having fun until Sunday on what I've found in my pocket – on precisely six pounds forty-two pence."

"Gosh, well, I'm hardly hungry at all," I lied. "What with the excitement of being here I couldn't eat a thing." I pointed down the boat to distract her from what was on the table. "I've made up the beds and put the stuff in the bathroom and put our clothes away. Come and look."

"Hmm," Mum said, looking at the bread. "I wonder if I can cut these down the middle and make ten thin slices out of five thick ones?"

"That would be good – narrowslices!" I

said. I laughed but Mum didn't so I went on, "The bathroom's really nice. It's got a corner bath and shower."

"A baked-bean omelette for supper, perhaps..."

"There's a hammock in one of the cupboards."

"And to follow, sardine." She frowned at me.

"Hannah's really enjoying herself. She's filled three pages of her birdy notebook already," I said, slightly niggled because my Spooky Seafaring Adventure Notebook had gone into the river with the other things.

Mum sighed heavily. "Well, I suppose we'd better get on. If I keep busy I might forget I'm hungry."

She went up the steps and a few moments later I heard the engine starting and off we went.

I stared out of the porthole, normally called a window. I wished it was beneath the waterline so I could look into the mysterious dark world under the river, but it just looked out on to fields. I frowned and concentrated like mad, but try as I might, I couldn't visualize a mermaid sitting out there. They didn't go with cows, somehow.

After a while Mum called. "I can see our first lock coming up, Amy. You and Hannah will have to help."

I sprang out, looking keen and unclumsy, ready to do my nautical best, and waved a hand in front of Hannah's face to bring her out of a duck-induced trance. The three of us then stood and stared, rather nervously, at what lay ahead.

"They're weird things, aren't they?" I said to Hannah. "Locks, I mean. I just can't work out how the river can be on two levels."

"I wonder if any birds go up and down just for a ride?" Hannah mused.

Mum stayed on the boat to steer it and call instructions to us, and Hannah and I got out and climbed up the little ladder at the side of the lock. We took a rope each at the front and back of the boat (fore and aft, as we say) and waited for the signal to pull. We were going into the lock with another narrowboat and a small, shiny white cruiser.

Under Mum's instructions we did all the negotiations beautifully:

pull forward slowly;

tie up;

get shouted at by lock-keeper;

untie;

move forward a little bit more;

get shouted at again by lock-keeper;

tie up – and so on, and then we got back on board and the gates closed behind us, boxing us in, and water started whooshing in, too, lifting us higher and higher.

When the water was all in, the front gates opened, Mum started the engine and we began to move off. The boat lurched and Hannah wobbled a bit and sat down heavily, holding on to the rail. "You haven't got your sea legs yet!" I called to her, and made a point of leaping gracefully down the boat to my place at the back.

I was a natural, I thought to myself, leaping like a young gazelle. And then my foot slipped and I lurched forward, over the rail and straight into the river.

Chapter 4

Friday Evening

....

"I've never been so embarrassed," Mum said. "There was I, trying to look capable and confident in front of the lock-keeper and *you* go head first overboard."

"It wasn't my—" I began.

"Not only that, but you went with such a splash that you practically drowned that couple in the white boat having their tea."

"I couldn't—"

"And then they had to haul you out and he got soaked all over again. The shame of it! First my handbag, then you!"

"It—"

"And the first thing the lock-keeper said was, 'that child should be wearing a life-jacket!'"

"I—"

"You also frightened a small flock of young mallards," Hannah said reproachfully.

"Huh!" I said, very fiercely to both of them, and then I went below deck to read my book. I was now dry, dressed and fastened into a life-jacket which Mum had laced so tightly I could hardly breathe.

I sat reading *Myths and Legends of the Sea* in dignified silence for about half an hour, and then Mum called me up on deck.

"There's a shop coming up on the right bank," she said, after checking me over to make sure the life-jacket was fastened tightly and I still wasn't able to breathe. "I'd like to go myself but I daren't leave you in charge of the boat. I'm going to give you half of our money, and you can go and buy us some food. Something sensible. Something filling."

"Okay," I said. "Are you coming, Hannah?"

"Hannah can do tomorrow's food run," Mum said. She raised her eyebrows at me. "We'll have a little competition to see who manages to get the most for their money."

* * *

The shop turned out to be a cross between a garage and a shed, just a big room filled with shelves which seemed to have everything in the world on them. Not just food, but, lined up in alphabetical order: ant-killer, aspirin, beeswax, bolts, cooking fuel, cotton reels and so on.

When I'd finished looking at everything (this took some time), I pressed the bell on the counter and, after a long wait, a woman appeared. I'd been hoping for someone extraordinary and interesting, but she was the wrong sort of extraordinary: she smelled funny and her hair was in tiny curlers all over her head.

"I'm in the middle of a perm," she said, "you'll have to be quick."

"I want to buy something to eat," I explained. "There's got to be a lot of it, and it's not to cost more than three pounds."

Her eyebrows raised themselves to the first line of curlers.

"What sort of something to eat?"

"Anything filling," I said, "where you get a lot for your money."

She shot over to a wire bin near the door and pulled out three large plastic bags of buns. "Marvellous value, these are. Twelve buns in each bag. You can have them for a pound a bag."

"Really?!" I said, amazed. That was twelve whole buns per person. Twelve great *big* buns.

"I'll take them," I said. As I was going out I happened to look down at the wire bin they'd been in and saw a notice stuck in the top. The cardboard was bent back so what I read was:

EED

UCKS

ITH

HESE

TALE

UNS!

and it took me until I got back to the *CC* to work out what the missing letters were.

Once I had, it was too late because Mum was saying, "Where on earth have you been. Hurry up!"

Half an hour down-river from the shop, we'd moored up again and were sitting round the table in the cabin ready to eat.

"What exactly did you buy?" Mum said. "I'm starving."

I put the buns on the table.

"Is that all?"

"All? There's loads here. You said to get as much as possible."

"I didn't mean in size." She sighed but began opening the nearest packet. "At least they'll fill us up." She put her hand in and pulled out a bun. "Or they would," she went on, "if we could get our teeth into them. They're stale! Hard as old boots! What's more," she said examining two of them closely. "Bits of them are green as well. Mouldy."

"Oops," I said.

Mum and I looked at each other. If we'd

been at home I'd have been given a severe shouting and told that I was absolutely *useless*. Because Hannah was with us, though, Mum just huffed, narrowed her eyes and muttered, "First my handbag. Then you falling in. Then this. I knew I shouldn't have trusted you." She handed over the buns to Hannah to feed the ducks with.

"I'd better not throw them," Hannah said, "if a duck got hit by one it could get a nasty headache." It was rather disloyal of her, I thought.

It was later, when we were moving again and I was helping her feed the ducks (after dipping the buns in the river to soggy them up) that I first noticed the mysterious phantom boat. It was getting dark and Mum had switched on our front light, but the mysterious phantom boat didn't have one so I couldn't make it out distinctly. Also I only caught the occasional glimpse of it. This might have been because it kept being hidden by the mist, or it might have been because it was a mysterious *disappearing* phantom boat.

Anyway, when I told Mum about it she said not to be so ridiculous and that she'd had quite enough of my goings-on, so I didn't say any more. I was just aware, with my specially sensitive powers, that it was there.

Chapter 5

Friday Night

I woke up to darkness and silence. Silence, that is, apart from something going *tap tap tap* at the porthole.

My eyes shot open. It had to be the phantom boat! It had pulled alongside and a phantom boatman was trying to come aboard!

I sat up and stared at the window. I could see the boatman's five fingers shining palely in the moonlight; five dead fingers tapping at the porthole!

"Eeek!" I said, several times, and "Agghh!"

When it became obvious that this wasn't going to wake Hannah, I stepped over and shook her. "Quick! Someone has risen from a watery grave and is trying to get in at the porthole!"

She woke up straight away. "Where?"

I pointed. "See, even as we speak, the hand

of death beckons!"

"It's a branch," she said, sliding down in her bed again, "and five willow leaves are brushing against the glass."

"Oh, well," I said. "I knew that really. I was just trying to have an adventure."

I knelt on her bunk and looked out of the porthole. There was no sign of the phantom boat.

"Actually," I went on excitedly, "there is a bit of an adventure out there, because the rope that's supposed to be holding our front end to the bank has come untied and we've drifted right out across the river."

"That's *your* rope," Hannah said. "You fastened the front, I did the back. You said you knew all the right knots to use."

"It was funny rope," I said. "I couldn't tie it properly."

"My knot hasn't come undone," she pointed out.

"Yes, well," I said. "I'd better get out there and fix it before Mum sees. If your end pulls away we'll be adrift. We could float down river and out to sea."

As I spoke, I thought, Mmm, I'd quite like that... I didn't think Mum would, though, so I pulled on my dressing gown. With a bit of luck I could get outside, get the rope, jump to shore and fix it and get back to bed without her knowing a thing about it.

"Your mum said you weren't to go on deck without your life-jacket," Hannah said.

"Oh, don't worry about that," I said. I slid open the trapdoor which led to the deck.

"She said—"

"I'll be perfectly all right," I said, climbing the ladder.

"But—"

"For goodness' sake!" I hissed back, "I am quite—" and then I stepped on to a little round thingy on the deck and fell backwards into the river.

"I'm perfectly all right," I said irritably. "I wouldn't have drowned, would I? I landed practically on the bank."

"In a metre of mud," Mum said, "which you have now managed to spread over the entire contents of this cabin." She gave a short scream. "It might be two o'clock in the morning but if the car was outside I'd just pack everything and go home, really I would. As if losing my handbag wasn't bad enough, now I have you *continually* falling in the river."

"Don't make such a fuss!" I said. "I'll just take all this stuff off, have a quick wash and get back into bed."

"And in the meantime, we're still half adrift!"

"Shall I go and fix the rope?" Hannah asked.

"No, I think I'd better do that myself," Mum said. She glowered at me. "Such a pity it wasn't done properly in the first place."

She went out to fix it while I had a shower and managed to coat most of the bath with mud. I went back to my bunk, only to find that (because I'd sat down on my bunk before I'd showered) the sheets had got themselves all muddied too.

"And the blankets are wet!" Mum said in a fierce whisper – the whisper was because Hannah had gone back to sleep.

"I could come in with you," I said, and as a panicky look came over Mum's face added quickly, "I could go in the hammock. It's in the cupboard and there's a sleeping bag with it."

Mum, sighing continually, got it out, and then we discovered that the only hanging points were above Hannah's bunk. She woke up once while we were fixing it, then again when I accidentally trod on her head, getting in.

At last, though, I was settled. I was in a sleeping bag and in the hammock and it was brilliant.

"I'm going back to bed now," Mum said, "and I don't want to hear a squeak out of you until at least nine o'clock in the morning. I'm on holiday too, remember?"

"I won't move; I won't do a thing," I said as she left, and I very gently pushed myself off the wall and began to sway from side to side.

This was more like it. This was proper Treasure Island seafaring stuff. I swayed faster and faster, left to right, right to left, until I felt seasick.

"Whee! Look at me!" I hissed to Hannah below.

"Go to sleep," she muttered.

"It's brilliant," I said, swinging madly from side to side. "Look – bet I can turn a full circle – loop the loop!"

"Bet you—*oouuff*!" she said, and the *oouuff* bit was because the hammock had broken right away from the wall and I'd fallen on her.

Chapter 6

Saturday Morning

"Well, what a lovely breakfast," Mum said sarcastically. "Sardine. Sardine on crust."

"It was all right," I said brightly. "If we want more I could catch sardines out of the river. All I need is a piece of string and a hook made out of a paperclip. That's what they use in books and they catch all sorts of things."

"Don't even think of it," Mum said. "You hanging over the edge of the boat *fishing* would be just asking for trouble."

"In one book," I went on, "the girl caught a trout – a special silver trout – and when it was slit open there was a great big pearl inside and it was worth millions of pounds."

"I thought you found pearls in oysters – not trout," Hannah said, managing to tear her glance away from the ducky things floating outside the window.

"No, the pearl was in there because the trout had swallowed it," I said. "People are always finding diamond rings in fish's insides – fish swallow valuable things all the time. I bet when people lose things overboard they get eaten up straight away."

"In that case," Mum said, "I wonder who's eaten my handbag?"

"Oh look!" I said quickly, pointing out of the window. "I think I can see the boat that's been following us – the phantom boat!"

Mum and Hannah both looked, but there was nothing there. I really thought I *had* seen something, though. A boat had disappeared behind a big clump of trees further down and not come out. It was definitely mysterious and I'd have put it in my notebook if I'd had it.

"There is no boat out there," Mum said and, seeing the mood she was in, I didn't dare contradict her. She began to clear away the plates.

"Hannah, I'm terribly sorry about this

starvation diet we seem to be on, I don't
know what your mum and dad will think."
She glowered at me. "If only Amy hadn't lost
my handbag."

"Oh, that's all right," Hannah said. She
patted the large plastic bag of bird food by
her side. "I've been snacking on these seeds
and nuts. They're quite nutritious."

"And so far you're not getting much sleep,
either," Mum went on. "I mean, when Amy's
not falling in the water in the middle of the
night, she's falling on you."

I ignored Mum and stared at the bag of
bird food. I could see peanuts in there, and
things that looked like dead cornflakes, and
stripy seeds and other things that might have
been currants. My mouth began to water;
sardine on crust hadn't exactly been a feast.

"Would you like me to help you feed the
ducks?" I asked Hannah. "It might be easier
– I could throw the seed while you watched
and took notes."

She moved slightly closer to the plastic bag.

"That's all right, thank you," she said. "The fewer people the better, really. Water birds tend to be shy."

"Well, I'll just come out and sit with you, shall I?" I said. Sit at the end of the boat ready to pounce on the birdseed. "I really feel quite interested in birds lately."

Mum and Hannah both looked at me.

"I do! I do!" I assured them. "I think birds are really ... really interesting."

Ten minutes later, yawning, I was trying to think of an excuse to get back to my book. I hadn't had a glimpse of the birdseed – I thought Hannah might be sitting on it – and I was getting hungrier by the minute. I'd shown some interest in a nice little fat brown and white duck which Hannah, encouraged by my curiosity, told me was a wigeon. She started rattling on about its breeding season and its habitat and all that, but I wasn't really listening. What I was thinking about was the time I'd been to a Chinese restaurant and had crispy duck in pancakes. I kept seeing this fat little wigeon served up with spring onion and a touch of soy sauce.

At lunchtime we stopped at another shop. It was Hannah's turn to buy the food and she went off while I helped Mum tie up our boat beside a posh blue and white cruiser. The cruiser had a little raised platform at the front, with a stripy awning over it, shading a dining table loaded with the remains of a meal. Five or six people were inside the cabin drinking out of tall glasses, but there was one woman still sitting at the table. She waved and said hello. I waved back as well as someone wearing a ridiculously tight life-jacket *could* wave.

Looking at all the stuff left on the table, my mouth began to water. There was half a cake, and a pile of sausage rolls, and a flan and some chicken legs and some cheese and...

Mum called me. "I want you to take our rubbish to the bins on shore, please," she said. "And MIND HOW YOU GO. I know you've got the life-jacket on, but I don't want any embarrassing incidents."

"I'll be perfectly all right," I said with dignity. Why did she have to go on all the time?

I looked again at the food on the next door table, then I waved to the woman again. "I'm just going to the rubbish bins," I said cheerily. "Can I take anything for you?"

"It's very nice of you to offer," the woman said, "but I'm too lazy to clear away yet."

"Leftover food does attract the flies," I murmured almost to myself.

"Oh, we've got a dog who'll finish up our leftovers in a trice," the woman said. "Thanks all the same."

I smiled falsely at her, my stomach giving a rolling squeal of hunger.

Mum shoved a black plastic bag of rubbish at me. "Nice try, Amy," she said through gritted teeth.

I looked at her. "I don't know what you mean."

"If you seriously thought I'd let you go

through a stranger's rubbish and eat the remains of their lunch..."

"Do you mind?" I said indignantly. "As if I'd do that. I don't know *how* you could think it."

Chapter 7

Saturday Afternoon

I came out of the willow-tree grotto I'd made
and glided towards where Hannah was lying
on the bank with her notebook.

"I am the Witch of the Water!" I cried
dramatically.

"Are you really?" Hannah said in a
whisper. "Could you be it quietly, then, so as
not to disturb the coots."

"Oh, all right," I said, flopping on to the
ground.

We were moored in an inlet a bit further on
from the food shop (where Hannah had
selected spagetti hoops and oven chips for
our lunch and so won the best-meal-for-least-
money game). We'd eaten, Mum was sitting
on the bank reading, Hannah was guess-
what-ing and I was being Witch of the Water.

I'd turned into one of these because there
was a willow on the bank which hung out

over the river, and I'd gone into the overhanging bit and fastened some of the branches together with hair bungees so it made a green and mysterious nook. I'd sat in there for a while looking for phantom boats, but because I wasn't actually sure what else a Witch of the Water did (and anyway, I betted they didn't do it whilst being strangled by a life-jacket) I'd got bored and gone to see what Hannah was up to.

"Want to come into my grotto?" I asked.

She shook her head. "Not now," she said in a whisper. "I've constructed this hide, you see, and I'm hoping to see a pochard."

"A pilchard?" I asked, and added wittily, "in tomato sauce?"

"A pochard," she said, staring intently over the river. "I'm sure I saw one earlier – the males have such striking plumage."

I looked all round. "Where's the hide, then?"

"You're lying on it," she said.

"Sorry!" I jumped up and tried to fluff out

the pile of dead grass. I made a show of watching the nearby ducks but they all looked the same; I was sure they were the ones that had been at the boatyard, following us. "Sure you don't want to come into my grotto, then?"

"Quite sure, thanks," she said, trying to look round me at the river.

"Well, if you change—"

"Hey! There's one!" she said in an excited whisper. "Over there – see its chestnut head?"

"Oh yes. Interesting," I said, and left her to it. I was used to Hannah. I quite liked having a friend who didn't like the same things as me and so didn't interfere with what I was doing, but sometimes I fancied having someone to talk to. Mum was no good – especially lately. All she wanted to do was talk about handbags.

I sat being green and mysterious in the grotto for a while longer, and then I wandered further down the river. It wasn't terrifically interesting. We'd come round a few bends so I couldn't see far, and there were no houses around. It was just green fields and the occasional boat.

I sat down on the bank and looked at my watch, wondering how long it was until dinnertime, and what we were having, when a dog came racing up. He was brown and white, small and sausage-shaped, with floppy ears.

I said hello to him and he bounded at me, so pleased to be spoken to that he almost bounced up and down on the spot. I threw sticks, he retrieved them, I rolled on the ground, he rolled with me, I paddled my feet in the water and so did he. Finally, I picked him up and he snuggled into me.

"Are you lost?" I said. "Have you fallen off a boat?"

Yes, he seemed to say. He looked up at me trustingly.

"Do you want me to help you get found again?"

He panted and closed his eyes. He was lost and exhausted, I decided. Exhausted from running after whichever boat he'd fallen off. And hungry too, no doubt. Well, I knew how he felt.

"What am I going to do with you?"

I chewed my lip. I couldn't just leave him here in the middle of nowhere. It might be days, weeks, before he was found again. I ought to get him on board and take him to the next boatyard – we'd be there tomorrow. But I couldn't just kidnap him, could I? Mum would go mad. Mind you, he'd be company for me while Hannah was looking at ducks.

I stroked his head and – well, I may have been imagining it but he seemed to smile at me. That decided it. I *couldn't* just leave him to starve.

So, what if I went back on board and he followed me? It wouldn't be my fault if he did that. If he stayed quiet all night, Mum probably wouldn't even know, and when we reached the boatyard in the morning he could just appear and the people there would know what to do with him. Whoever had lost him would probably have reported it by then and there might be a big reward.

So I'd just go aboard, I decided, and see if he came with me. I patted his little fat tummy, thinking that it was a pity he wasn't a hound from hell, but you couldn't have everything. I'd call him Baskerville, in any case.

I put him down and he looked at me miserably, as if I'd rejected him. I began to walk very slowly back to the boat and he followed at my heel. He was so small, he was almost hidden by the long grass along the bank.

Whistling casually, I passed within a few feet of Hannah and approached the boat. Mum was sitting in a chair on the riverbank with her nose in a book, and didn't even notice I was around.

I went on board and Baskerville followed. I

didn't give him any encouragement, apart from a quick "Here, boy!" a couple of times.

I went below deck and he pattered down the stairs behind me and went straight to the space under my bunk where ropes and stuff were stored. He used the hinged flap like a doggy-door. As if he knew; as if he'd been there before. It was just as well he wasn't a hound from hell, because if he was he'd never have fitted into such a small space.

Well, that was decided, then. He'd come aboard all on his own and it wasn't anything to do with me.

I put a saucer of water under the bunk, thinking that I'd worry about his food later, when I worried about mine. I stretched out on top of the bunk and started reading.

Half an hour later Mum came on board and called down to me that we were going to get moving. She said that there was a big pub that served food further on and she wanted to tie up there and see if she could bargain with them to get an evening meal.

"What – you mean we'll eat and wash up afterwards?" I asked.

"Of course not!" Mum said. "I mean I'll leave something there – my watch or a ring – and then come back in the week and pay properly. It'll be *so* embarrassing but this is what I'm reduced to, seeing as you've lost my h—"

"I'm going to call Hannah," I said, charging up the stairs to escape the "h" word.

When Hannah was back (and I'd checked that Baskerville was still there) she and I did our bit with the ropes, then Mum started the engine and off we went.

We'd hardly got going when, just as we were passing under a bridge, I saw the boat – the phantom boat – coming along behind us.

"That boat's there!" I called to Mum excitedly. "Look behind before it disappears again!"

She slowed right down and looked, letting it get closer. Then she saw who it was.

"It's him – the boatyard man!" she called.

"What a cheek! He's following us!"

Hannah and I looked, and it was him all right, standing on the front of the *Esmerelda*.

"Not a phantom boat at all," I said, disappointed. Only *him* – what a swindle. The holiday would be over the next day and not a single spooky seafaring adventure had occurred.

"No phantom," Mum said fiercely. "Just that awful man trying to check up on us."

"He's waving. Beckoning," Hannah said. "And shouting something."

"He can jolly well shout for all he's worth," Mum said, "but I won't be here to listen to him." She pushed the thingy forward and we shot off. "Full steam ahead, everyone!"

Chapter 8

Saturday Evening

"Well, we seem to have shaken him off," Mum said as we moored by a sign which said: *The Jolly Water Rat*. "I'm glad I insisted on keeping the faster boat."

"You drive boats really well, Mum," I said smarmily. "You're a natural."

I was being smarmy because I knew what was coming. Sure enough, a moment later she said, "Well, I suppose I'd better go into this pub and get it over with."

"It looks a really nice place," I said, peering out of the porthole towards the *The Jolly Water Rat*.

She tutted. "It's not every woman who has to go and exchange her most treasured possessions for food."

I smiled cheerily and swung my feet up on my bunk. "I bet they do really good food there. What d'you fancy to eat, Hannah?"

"Of course," Mum went on, "I wouldn't have to go through this ordeal if it hadn't been for a certain someone dropping my—"

I was taken with a sudden attack of coughing, partly to stop her saying the dreaded word and partly to cover the scuffling which had broken out under my bunk. My stowaway was getting restless.

"That's quite a cough. I expect you're going down with something," Mum said. "Can't say I'm surprised: you've been more or less permanently in the water ever since we've been here."

"I've only been in twice," I said, and I swung my feet down again and started drumming them on the floor loudly. "And anyway, that was before I was an experienced sailor. Do I have to keep wearing this life-jacket?"

"Yes, you most certainly do."

"It's so tight it restricts my blood flow," I said. "And when I try to eat wearing it, my food won't go down my tubes."

"It's lucky we haven't had much food, then," Mum said. She sighed in annoyance at the din. "Do you have to do that?"

I carried on drumming, pretending I didn't know what she was talking about. While I drummed I made sure my feet were in front of the trap door so that Baskerville couldn't get out.

"I should go before it gets crowded, Mum," I said. "It looks the sort of pub that would get really busy on a Saturday night."

"Oh yes," Mum said, "there's a whole flotilla of boats tying up outside, isn't there?"

But she was hungry so she went. And I stopped drumming.

After a moment, Hannah, without looking up from her book, said, "What's that noise, Amy?"

"What noise?"

"A scuffling. Like some sort of animal."

"Just the dog," I said.

She looked up. "What dog?"

"The ship's dog. Baskerville."

"Oh," she said.

I moved my feet away from the doggy door and out he shot.

"It *is* a dog!" Hannah said. "I thought you were making it up – that it was one of your stories. How did he get here?"

I put on my do-gooding expression. Or possibly my *dog*-gooding expression. "It's a poor little lost doggy that I found wandering alone on the riverbank."

"But what's he doing under your bunk?"

"I rescued him. I'm taking him back to civilization."

She looked at me, alarmed. "Your mum will go mad."

"She won't know," I said. "When we get to the boatyard in the morning I'll let him out and then the people there will look after him and find his owners."

"But you can't just pick up a dog on a riverbank and take it away!"

"I told you – he was lost," I said. "Anyway, I couldn't help it, there was nothing I could do. He forced his way on board."

We both stared at Baskerville, who was sitting there wagging his tail, looking about as forceful as a fluffy bunny.

"I see," she said. "And what's he going to eat?"

"Some of our dinner," I said.

"Some of *your* dinner," she said.

Mum was away for fifteen minutes, which gave me time to take Baskerville for a walk along the riverbank. I was regretting having rescued him, actually. He was turning out to be more trouble than he was worth.

Mum brought fish and chips back to the boat, having left her wristwatch there in temporary payment, and while we were eating I managed to stuff a few chips up my sleeve. I motioned to Hannah to do the same but she pretended not to understand.

When Mum went back to get the hot apple pies she'd arranged for us to have for pudding, I fed Baskerville the chips and persuaded Hannah to part with some of the bigger, more biscuity bits of bird food. I then tried to teach him some tricks, but he escaped under the bunk, so I let him be. He seemed to like it under there.

Hannah was writing in her birdy notebook so, casting about for something to do, something which had a touch of seafaring adventure about it, I decided to write a message and put it in a bottle.

Mum was ages (we found out later that she'd eaten her apple pie there) so I had time to cunningly age a piece of notepaper so it looked like old parchment. I then wrote, in wriggly, quavery handwriting, a curious and intriguing message: *Who releases me releases the spirit of the deep.* I thought that that would give someone a nice fright. I sealed up the curious and intriguing message in an empty tomato sauce bottle I found under the sink.

I was just about to throw it overboard when Mum came back with our apple pies on little cardboard plates. We ate them and then she said she wanted to get moving straight away, before it got really dark, so it was full speed ahead again.

I was dying to throw my bottle in the water. I went to stand behind Mum, where she couldn't see me, whirled it round my head and chucked it down river as far as I could.

There was a moment's silence during which I imagined it whizzing through the air, then came the faint sound of smashing glass, swiftly followed by a distant angry roar.

When I peered through the gloom I could just make out the *Esmerelda* with Mr Boatyard on the front, a very angry Mr Boatyard, rubbing his head and leaping up and down.

I dropped like a stone to the deck.

"What *are* you doing?" Mum asked as I crawled on all fours towards the cabin.

"Just getting out of your way," I said. "Wind resistance and all that. If I keep down you'll be able to go faster."

Chapter 9

Sunday Morning

I spent the next morning trying to keep out of Mum's way as much as possible, whilst trying to plan how I was going to get Baskerville off the *CC* without her noticing.

We'd been going at full pelt since it was light, with Hannah duck-detecting in all directions and Mum going on and on about hot baths, having me underfoot, what a fine holiday this was and how she hadn't been able to relax for a moment since we'd set off. All this moaning on her part made me wonder how she'd have coped if we'd been on a proper ship for months and years on end with sharks and waves as high as houses and all those sorts of things. Well, she just *wouldn't* have coped, would she?

As the boatyard came into view I heard her call, "At last! I could cry with relief!" which I thought was rather over the top. I put a welly against the doggy door and went on deck.

"I can take this thing off now, can't I?" I said, picking open the strings of the life-jacket.

"No, you CANNOT."

"But I'm perfectly safe now!" I pleaded.

"That thing will *not* be taken off until we are at least ten miles from any water."

"But I'm used to the river now."

"Amy!"

"I'm hardly going to—"

Just as I was speaking, the *CC* bumped hard against a wall. I lurched sideways, grabbed at a rail which gave way and went head first in a spectacular dive into the river.

It was a boatyard *lady* at this end, and when I bobbed up to the top of the water she poked a long pole at me which hooked my life-jacket, and hauled me on to the quay. I felt like one of those yellow plastic ducks with a number on its bottom that you hook out at the fair.

"I'm *so* sorry," Mum was saying in a nice

voice in one direction, "I really can't apologize enough." In the other direction and in a fierce voice she was saying, "Really, Amy, I just can't believe it!" and "Never again!"

"It wasn't my fault," I said as she prodded me below deck to change into what I could find in the way of dry clothes. "You bumped the boat. *Anyone* would have gone over the side, the way it lurched."

"Wherever *you* go, there's trouble ... incidents ... disturbances." As she said each word she rubbed my hair with a towel in a wicked way, so that it pulled and tangled.

Dryish and stuffed into my life-jacket again, I sighed. A whole weekend on the rolling river and not a single adventure. No mainbraces had been spliced (whatever that meant) no lost country beneath the waters had been discovered, we hadn't even been invaded by giant crabs.

"I'm so happy I saw a shoveler," Hannah said while she was gathering her things together, and I thought how easily pleased she was – excited just because she'd seen an old bird. It was much more difficult being me; my kind of excitement didn't come along nearly so often.

Mum, after one last shout at me, said she was going to arrange for our lift back to the first boatyard. She disappeared into the office with Mrs Boatyard and I went below deck to get Baskerville out.

"What are you doing with him now?" Amy said.

I grinned. "I'm taking him off. Disembarking him. Disem*bark*ing him! Get it?"

Hannah didn't laugh. Instead she said, "Oh look, Amy, it's that boat again!" and I turned to see the *Esmerelda* coming towards us with Mr Boatyard, stony-faced, at the helm.

Mum must have seen him too because she came straight out of the office before I'd had a chance to get rid of Baskerville. By the time she reached us, Mr Boatyard had tied up and was striding over with a fierce expression on his face. I, thinking of the curious-and-intriguing-message-in-a-bottle incident, thought it might be as well to disappear, but Mum said, "OK, you two girls. I want you to back me up in everything I say," so I couldn't.

Mum stood on the front of the *CC* looking – as I told her – as brave and fearless as a ship's figurehead. I tried to hide behind Hannah and rehearsed saying, "Bottle? What bottle?"

Mr Boatyard came up breathing fire. But Mum was breathing fire too, and got going first.

"I don't know *what* you think you've been doing, pursuing a woman and two innocent children," she said, "but let me tell you I think your behaviour is utterly despicable!"

He was completely taken aback.

"We managed the boat with complete competence," Mum went on. "There was absolutely no reason for you to trail us as if we were a bunch of inept simpletons who were going to crash or fall overboard at any moment!" I stepped slightly more behind Hannah, hoping he wouldn't notice that my hair was wet.

"But I merely—"

"As it was, we were frightened and alarmed by you at every turn. The two children have been unable to sleep at night, thinking we were being pursued by axe-wielding maniacs!"

"Phantoms from the deep, actually," I put in softly.

"Madam, I—"

As he spoke, there was a sudden, sharp bark from below deck.

"What's that?" he and Mum said together.

I considered doing one of my imitation dog barks but thought better of it. No one said anything and Baskerville barked again.

"It's a dog," Hannah blurted out.

"What dog?" Mum and Mr Boatyard said together again.

"A ship's dog," said Hannah, and she

nudged me to speak.

But Mr Boatyard yelled, "Skipper!" and there was a wuffing and a scuffling from below deck and suddenly Baskerville shot up the stairs. He leapt across to Mr Boatyard, who picked him up and got licked all over his face. He looked at Mum coldly while he was being licked. "So you thought that as well as insulting me, you'd help yourself to my dog, did you?"

"I most certainly did not help myself to your dog," Mum said indignantly. "I don't even like dogs. I have never seen this dog before in my life."

"This dog, Madam, was on your boat. Are you pretending that you didn't know it was there?"

"I am not pretending that I—"

I sighed heavily. Unless I spoke up we were going to be here for hours. And I was absolutely starving.

When I sighed, they both looked at me.

I stepped forward. "I rescued that dog," I

said. "It was on the riverbank, lost and alone, miles from anywhere. I took it on board and saved its life."

"Amy!" Mum said.

"That dog," Mr Boatyard said, "knows every inch of the river – and every inch of your boat, come to that. He was merely taking exercise from my boat, which was probably moored down-river to yours."

He turned to Mum. "May I suggest, Madam, that—"

"Oh, do stop calling me Madam," Mum interrupted. She turned to me and narrowed her eyes to slits: wait-till-I-get-you-home slits. "This is just an unfortunate misunderstanding," she went on. "My daughter obviously thought the dog was lost and ... er ... as she's a sensitive child, she decided to do what she could to help. It was a well-meaning gesture which went wrong."

I beamed. I couldn't have put it better myself.

"And was throwing a bottle that hit me on

the head another well-meaning gesture from a sensitive child?" Mr Boatyard demanded.

I tried to slip sideways but Mum put out a hand to restrain me. A tight, gripping sort of hand.

"But before we come to that," Mr Boatyard said, "perhaps I might be allowed to say the following. I was not pursuing you trying to catch you out, I merely wanted to return this." From the canvas holdall slung over his shoulder, he pulled out – Mum's handbag! "You carelessly left it in my office," he went on, "and I thought you might need it."

Mum was speechless for a moment, then she said, "Oh ... I ..."

When I looked at her she'd gone bright red.

"As I believe I mentioned, the *Esmerelda* is slower than the *Cheeky Chappie*, but it so happened that I had to return her to this boatyard anyway so I thought I'd take your handbag along and try and catch you up."

"Oh my..." Mum said.

"I didn't drop it!" I shrieked, suddenly

finding my voice. "I *knew* I didn't drop it!"

She ignored me. "I really don't know what to say. I'm terribly sorry, Mr Boatyard ... er ..."

"Richard," said Mr Boatyard.

"It was *you* all the time, Mum!" I said. "You left it there. I knew I didn't drop it!"

Mum stopped me with a glint. "I'd just like to apologize for causing you so much trouble, Richard, and to thank you very much for trying to return my bag. The thing that's worrying me is, what did you mean about being hit on the head with a bottle?"

I swiftly weighed up my options. There was the Baskerville incident on the downside, against the handbag incident on the upside. But the bottle incident – well, that was something else, that was going to take quite a bit of getting out of.

"Look," I said, "it can all be explained." As I spoke I stepped forward, wringing my hands and trying to look anxious, remorseful and sorrowful. Unfortunately I was so busy concentrating on this that I forgot to look where I was stepping. I tripped over a coil of rope, shouted "Ooops!" and (under the circumstances I think it was the best thing I could have done) fell in.